This Book Belongs to

_____

For Pat,
this is a thing I know.

Copyright © 2021 by Emily Winfield Martin

All rights reserved. Published in the United States by Random House Children's Books,
a division of Penguin Random House LLC, New York.

Random House and the colophon are registered trademarks of Penguin Random House LLC.

Visit us on the Web! rhcbooks.com

Educators and librarians, for a variety of teaching tools, visit us at RHTeachersLibrarians.com

Library of Congress Cataloging-in-Publication Data
Names: Martin, Emily Winfield, author, illustrator.
Title: This is a gift for you / Emily Winfield Martin.
Description: First edition. | New York : Random House Children's Books, [2021] | Audience: Ages 3–7. |
Summary: Illustrations and simple, rhyming text reveal a parent's wishes for a child,
such as being alone and not alone, quiet and loud, enjoying moments shared, just the two of them.
Identifiers: LCCN 2020046335 | ISBN 978-1-5247-1416-1 (hardcover) |
ISBN 978-1-5247-1417-8 (library binding) | ISBN 978-1-5247-1418-5 (ebook)
Subjects: CYAC: Stories in rhyme. | Parent and child—Fiction.
Classification: LCC PZ8.3.M41852 | DDC [E]—dc23

The text of this book is set in 28-point Centaur MT Pro.
The illustrations in this book were created using acrylic, gouache, and colored pencil.
Book design by Nicole de las Heras
MANUFACTURED IN CHINA
10 9 8 7 6 5 4 3 2 1
First Edition

This is a Gift for You

Emily Winfield Martin

Random House New York

This is a gift for you:

Just something
little
and out
of the blue.

This is a thing that's true:

The best treasures fit

in a pocket

(or two).

This is a thing
I know:

If we watch

The world closely . . .

Magic

will show.

So I'll give you this world
Like a lucky blue stone. . . .

The gift of alone . . .

And
not-being-alone.

The gift of quiet . . .

And the gift of loud . . .

Your hand in my hand

Out in a crowd.

The gift of *Sorry* when we're wrong.

The gift of singing your favorite song.

The gift of knowing you
Better than most . . .

The gift of

Seven kinds of toast.

A place to dream . . .

A place to *Do*

A place for perfectly imperfect you.

A warm place after you wander all day . . .

And a light in the dark

To guide your way.

Because this is a thing that's true:

Days that should never end usually do.

This is a thing I know:
My arms are somewhere
You always can go.

This is a gift of our own,
Just two little people
On a lucky blue stone.

I want a forever

Of moments like these.

But this is
a gift, here, just
you and me.

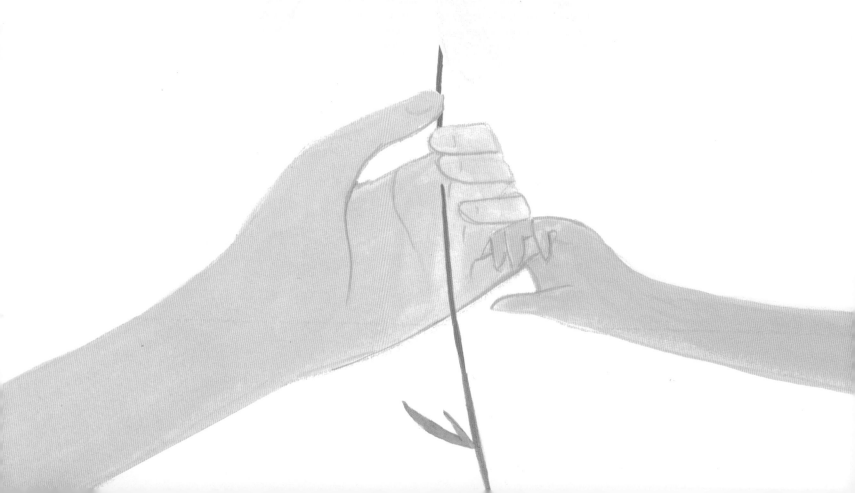